Everyone's Singing, Lord

38 children's songs for collective worship

Compiled by Sue Fearon
Illustrated by Rachel Fuller and Carla Moss

Sung by Zoe Tyler
Arranged and recorded by Note-orious Productions Ltd

A&C Black • London

First published 2003
by A&C Black Publishers Ltd
an imprint of Bloomsbury Publishing Plc
50 Bedford Square, London, WC1B 3DP
© 2003 A&C Black Publishers Ltd
Reprinted 2013

This book is produced using paper that is made from wood
grown in managed, sustainable forests. It is natural, renewable
and recyclable. The logging and manufacturing processes
conform to the environmental regulations of the country of
origin.

Book/CD pack: ISBN 978-1-4081-9696-0

Cover illustration and inside design by Carla Moss
Cover design by
Inside illustrations by Rachel Fuller and Carla Moss © 2003
Edited by Katherine Kermode and Sheena Roberts
Music set by Jeanne Fisher
CD produced by Andrew Lynwood
Performed by Zoe Tyler
Accompaniments arranged and recorded by Note-orious
Productions Ltd

Printed in Great Britain by Martins the Printers Ltd,
Berwick upon Tweed

contents

CD track numbers are the same as song numbers

Creation and natural world

Thanks and praise

Prayer songs

Introduction

Planning an act of collective worship which has a broadly Christian character and yet is truly collective (enabling every member of the school community to be present and have the opportunity to participate) can prove challenging. The purpose of this book is to make that task easier.

'Collective worship in schools should aim to provide the opportunity for pupils to worship God, to consider spiritual and moral issues and to explore their own beliefs: to encourage participation and response through active involvements in the presentation of worship or through listening to and joining in the worship offered: and to develop community spirit, promote a common ethos and shared values, and reinforce positive attitudes.' Circular 1/94 paragraph 50
School Standards and Framework Act 1999

Everyone's singing, Lord is a collection of 38 songs which have been carefully chosen to provide a new and exciting source of material for collective worship. Each song is accompanied by notes which give guidance to the teacher and provide both presentation ideas and prayer themes. The musical arrangements are straightforward, but the accompanying performance CD makes it possible to learn the songs even if the school has no pianist.

Parents have the right to withdraw their children from daily acts of collective worship. However, in most schools there is a desire that the whole school community gathers together for this important part of school life. Consequently, the language used in acts of collective worship needs to enable people from a variety of different backgrounds to worship God together. The songs in this book have been carefully selected and are expected to be suitable for use in almost all schools. Where there are words in individual songs which it may not be appropriate to ask those of all religious backgrounds to sing, the guidance notes will alert teachers. The guidance notes in this book are included to help those who lead acts of collective worship to select songs which are suitable for each particular school.

An act of worship which is wholly or broadly of a Christian character will typically centre on Jesus, as Jesus is the centre of the Christian faith. This might involve an aspect of Jesus' life, an element of his teaching or simply the way in which an Old Testament passage points forward to Jesus' coming. In my experience, there are many teachers who feel nervous of talking about Jesus in school because the pupils are drawn from a variety of faith backgrounds. But, if the teaching is presented as 'what Christians believe' or as something 'which the Bible says', children who are not practising Christians are able to hear the teaching without feeling pressured by it. We can never 'make' anyone worship, but we should create the opportunity for those who want to worship to do so.

Some teachers express reservations about leading collective worship for another reason: a lack of Christian faith and, or knowledge. The talking points and prayer ideas have been included as a resource for those teachers who are not familiar with a wide variety of material for Christian worship and to assist them in building an integrated assembly despite the busy schedule. Bible references have also been included to ensure that a favourite Bible story can be quickly found. Often the story can be most accessible to children in a modern translation and the web site *www.biblegateway.com* gives ready access to a wide variety of translations. You might try looking up the story in the *New International Version* (NIV-UK) or for more child-friendly language try the *Contemporary English Version* (CEV) or *The Message* (MSG).

In monotheistic religions (eg Christianity, Judaism and Islam) it is generally acceptable to pray to God by a variety of titles, but not to use the personal name for God adopted by another religion. So to ensure worship is always collective and appropriate to individual children's cultural and faith backgrounds, please invite children to join in with the prayer only if they want to.

When introducing prayer you may wish to say 'I am going to talk to God. If you agree with what I say you can join in with the Amen at the end, because Amen basically means 'Yes, I agree''.

As the children of your school join together in song, it is hoped that they will indeed learn to share a common ethos, a peace, joy and confidence built upon their knowledge and worship of God.

Sue Fearon

Sue Fearon works for Birmingham City Mission as a children's worker, conducting assemblies and lessons in primary schools throughout the city.

acknowledgements

Grateful acknowledgement is made to the following who have granted permission for the reprinting of copyright material:

Father God, you love me words and music by Paul Crouch and David Mudie; *Father, I thank you* words and music by Yvonne Scott; © 1993 Daybreak Music Ltd, PO Box 2848, Eastbourne, BN20 7X, info@daybreakmusic.co.uk. All rights reserved. International copyright secured.

For God so loved the world words and music by John Hardwick, © 1992 Daybreak Music Ltd, PO Box 2848, Eastbourne, BN20 7X, info@daybreakmusic.co.uk. All rights reserved. International copyright secured. Used by permission.

Just a tiny seed words and music by Tracey Atkins, Richard Atkins and Andrew Pratt, © 1995 Stainer & Bell Ltd, London, England and The Trustees for Methodist Church Purposes.

Like a candle flame words and music by Graham Kendrick © 1988 Make Way Music. www.grahamkendrick.co.uk.

My God is so big words and music by Ruth Harms Calkin © 1986 Nuggets of Truth BMI.

Nobody's a nobody words and music by John Hardwick, © 1993 Daybreak Music Ltd, PO Box 2848, Eastbourne, BN20 7X, info@daybreakmusic.co.uk. All rights reserved. International copyright secured. Used by permission.

Now and forever words and music by Ruth Wills, © 1994 Saltmine.

O Lord, hear my prayer music by Jacques Bethier, © Ateliers et Presses de Taize, 71250 Taize-Community, France.

One more to count words and music by Alan and Eileen Simmons, © 2001 Alan Simmons Music, PO Box 7, Scissett, Huddersfield, HD8 9YZ.

Our Father in heaven words and music by Sheila Wilson, © 1999 Redhead Music Limited, from 'New Millennium Heroes!'

Special words and music by Paul Field, © 1991 Daybreak Music Ltd, PO Box 2848, Eastbourne, BN20 7X, info@daybreakmusic.co.uk. All rights reserved. International copyright secured. Used by permission.

Every effort has been made to trace and acknowledge copyright owners. If any right has been omitted, the publishers offer their apologies and will rectify this in subsequent editions following notification.

The following have been commissioned and composed especially for Everyone's Singing, Lord.

A prayer in times of uncertainty words and music by Julia Wagstaff, © 2003 Julia Wagstaff, A&C Black Publishers Ltd.

Endless praise words from Psalm 8, music by David Stoll, © 2003 David Stoll, A&C Black Publishers Ltd.

Everywhere Around Me Words and music by Mark and Helen Johnson, from 'Songs for Every Assembly', © 1998 & 2008 Out of the Ark Ltd, Middlesex, TW12 2HD CCLI Song No: 2642310

Harvest thanks words by Christina Lane, music traditional. Words © 2003 Christina Lane, A&C Black Publishers Ltd.

Morning's here words and music by David Stoll, © 2003 David Stoll, A&C Black Publishers Ltd.

He doesn't look like a king and *In the light* words and music by Susannah Pearse, © 2003 Susannah Pearse, A&C Black Publishers Ltd.

Like the wise men of old words and music by Sheila Wilson, © 2003 Sheila Wilson, Redhead Music Ltd, A&C Black Publishers Ltd.

Peace words and music by Ruth Wills, © 2003 Ruth Wills, A&C Black Publishers Ltd.

Safe with the Lord words and music by Dot Fraser, © 2003 Dot Fraser, A&C Black Publishers Ltd.

Shout for joy words Psalm 100, music by Peter Readman, © 2003 Note-orious Productions Ltd, A&C Black Publishers Ltd.

Song of Blessing Words and music by Mark and Helen Johnson, from 'Songs for Every Assembly', © 1998 & 2008 Out of the Ark Ltd, Middlesex, TW12 2HD CCLI Song No: 2540065

The Lord is my shepherd words Psalm 23, music by Peter Readman, © 2003 Note-orious Productions Ltd, A&C Black Publishers Ltd.

The man from Galilee words and music by Sue Fearon, music traditional, © 2003 Sue Fearon, A&C Black Publishers Ltd.

The most magnificent pizza words by Christina Lane, music traditional. Words © 2003 Christina Lane, A&C Black Publishers Ltd.

The senses song words and music by Ruth Wills and Phil Brown, © 1994 Saltmine.

Walk in peace words and music by Stephen Chadwick, © 2003 Stephen Chadwick, A&C Black Publishers Ltd

The following stories are by Steve Stickley: *The long-spooned café, Spludge, Frankie and the baby, The sparrow, the cockerel, the crow and the dove, Bella's lunch, Will we ever stop fighting?* and *The pit stop* © 2003 Steve Stickley, A&C Black publishers Ltd.

The following stories are by Carla Moss: *Small, When the storm rose up* and *Rich* © 2003 Carla Moss, A&C Black publishers Ltd.

The following story is from the Reverend Michael Schaeffer, CESA: *Nkosi* © 2003 the Reverend Michael Schaeffer, A&C Black publishers Ltd.

The following poem is by Charlie McCarthy: *Banded* © 2003 Charlie McCarthy, A&C Black publishers Ltd.

Alleluia words and music anon; *Be still and know* words and music anon; words for verse 3 by Sue Fearon; *Breton fisherman's prayer* words and music traditional; *Dansai* words and music traditional Ghanaian; *Halle, hallelujah!* Words traditional, music anon; *I love the pit, pit, patter* words of verse 1 and music traditional, words for verses 2 and 3 by Sue Fearon; *Siya hamba* words and music traditional African and *Who made the rolling sea?* Words and music traditional. These arrangements © A&C Black publishers Ltd.

The compiler and publishers would also like to thank the following people who have generously assisted in the preparation of this book: Marianne Beha, Jenny Fisher, Dot Fraser, Helen Gaitenby, Christian Hron, Charlie McCarthy, Alison Mitchell, Carla Moss, Marie Penny, Peter Readman, Rev. Michael Shaeffer, Jane Sebba, Steve Stickley, Barbara Thomas, Zoe Tyler and Ivy Lane Primary School, Chippenham, Wiltshire; Stanton St Quinton CE Primary School, Wiltshire.

1. Everywhere around me

Words and music by Mark and Helen Johnson
From 'Songs for Every Assembly' by Mark and Helen Johnson © Out of the Ark Music

1 Tell me who made all of creation,
  Who designed the wonders of nature?
  Whose idea was pattern and colour,
  Wonderful to see?

Chorus

Ev'rywhere around me,
  I can see the hand of God,
The evidence surrounds me,
  In the greatness of his world.
Ev'rywhere around me,
  I can see the hand of God,
The evidence surrounds me,
  In the greatness of his world.

2 Tell me who made music and laughter,
  Who designed our bodies to start with?
  Whose idea was thinking and feeling,
  Who gave life to me?
  Chorus

3 Don't stop looking, don't stop believing,
  God is to be found when you seek him.
  All creation tells of his glory,
  For eternity.
  Chorus

Ev'rywhere around me!

Chorus

-round me,　　　　　　　　I can see the hand_ of God.___

___　The ev-i-dence sur-rounds me,　　In the

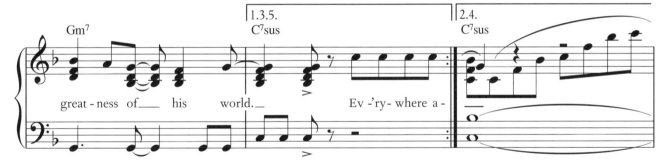

great-ness of___ his world.___　Ev-'ry-where a-

ff Ev-'ry-where a-round　me!

Guidance note:
The Bible says that God made the whole universe (Genesis 1). Belief in God as the creator is common to many faiths.

Christian talking point:
Creation is one of the ways in which we can appreciate the greatness of God. Encourage the children to picture a being who is great enough to make the sun, moon and stars, and who also loves and cares for each one of us. (Bible reference: Psalm 8; verses 3 and 4).

General talking point:
The time and thought we spend on creating things makes them precious to us. Ask the children to think about something they have enjoyed making recently and why. How would they like other people to treat things that they had made? Encourage them to think about how they treat the world and to respect and care for it in a similar way.

Reflection:

Banded
by Charlie McCarthy

From deep within the ground
comes the
banded chalcedony.
With rings of
pink
peach
grey
white
black
and threads of red.

My fingerprints are mine alone.
Like you and me the agate rings
Will never be the same.

So good to hold.
So warm to take.
Safe, calm and special
In the palm of my hand.

© 2003 Charlie McCarthy, A&C Black Publishers Ltd

Prayer:
Dear God, thank you for making the world and everything in it. Thank you for making so much variety and detail. Please remind us to look at and enjoy all the wonderful things you have created. AMEN

2. This beautiful world

Words and music by Debbie Campbell
© 2003 Debbie Campbell, A&C Black Publishers Ltd

1 Everywhere we go trees and flowers grow.
 Nature's bountiful rivers gently flow,
Giving us a green and pleasant land,
 A friend on whom we can depend.
Look around and what do we see?
 Nature's perfect harmony.
Makes us all so thankful we can be
 A part of this beautiful world.

2 Somewhere far away, people everyday
 Watch their crops and their forests waste away,
Praying for a green and pleasant land,
 A friend on whom they can depend.
Look around and what do they see?
 Famine, drought and poverty.
Makes them ask how ever can it be
 A part of this beautiful world?

3 People everywhere, if we learn to care,
 We will see there is food enough to share,
Living in a green and pleasant land,
 A friend on whom we can depend.
Living in a green and pleasant land,
 A friend on whom we can depend.

Guidance note:
This song raises moral and environmental issues.

Christian talking point:
The Bible says that God created a perfect world (Genesis 1) and yet today we see famine, drought and poverty. We struggle to understand why many have food to waste when others starve. If the whole of creation was 'good' when God made it, what went wrong? Why? Can we make a difference?

General talking point:
For a class assembly discuss how the food production and national wealth of any country may be affected by unexpected weather, eg drought, hurricanes, flooding. Can any of the parents contribute stories about how the weather has had a dramatic impact on them or their families?

Story:
The Long-Spooned Café by Steve Stickley

There was a cook who made the most magnificent and exquisite meals. The colours were rich and magnificent. The tastes were so scrummy they were out of this world. One night the cook had a strange dream that her wonderful dishes were to be served in The Long-Spooned Café, a peculiar eating place where customers could only use long-handled spoons.

She set about creating beautiful meals of rich meats and succulent fruits, such as you couldn't imagine. Then the food was served to her hungry customers. The first lot tried picking up the food with the spoons but couldn't get it to their mouths because the handles were far too long. Food splattered everywhere – it was trodden into the carpets, it slid down the walls, the customers were extremely annoyed and went home hungry. Some even started fighting. It was horrendous.

The second lot of customers in her dream also sat down to her gorgeous meal, but instead of being unable to eat, they came out of the café some time later completely delighted, having feasted upon the cook's wonderful food. The cook woke up laughing and full of admiration.

What do you think the second lot of customers did differently?
(Answer: they fed each other)

© 2003 Steve Stickley, A&C Black Publishers Ltd

Prayer:
Dear God, help us to understand why some people have plenty to eat while others have very little. Please help us always to be grateful for what we enjoy and to share what we have with each other. AMEN

3. who made the rolling sea?

Words and music traditional
This arrangement © 2003 A&C Black Publishers Ltd

1 Who made the rolling sea,
   The rolling sea, the rolling sea?
Who made the rolling sea?
   Our Father God.

2 Who made the stars that shine?
   ...Our Father God.

3 Who made the birds that fly?
   ...Our Father God.

4 Who made you and me?
   ...Our Father God.

Our Father God

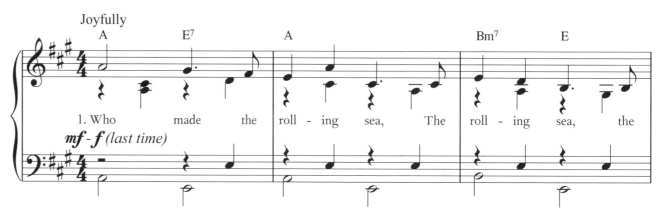
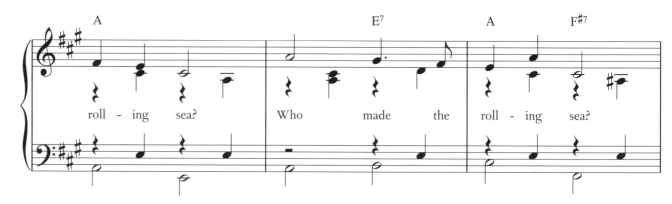
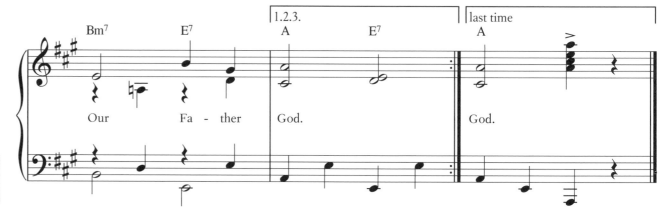

Guidance note:
This very simple song is suitable for even the youngest children, and states the God-centred view of creation adopted by the major world religions.

Christian talking point:
Astronomers have calculated that there are more stars in the universe than grains of sand on Earth. The Bible says that God not only made the stars but 'calls each one by name.' (Bible reference: Psalm 147:4.)

Reflection:
Ask the children to picture one thing in the world (stars, fish in the sea, birds, people or anything else) and to contemplate their number and variety.

Prayer:
Dear God, we look at the stars and think of their number and they remind us of your greatness. AMEN

4. Father, I thank you

Words and music by Yvonne Scott
© 1993 Daybreak Music Ltd, PO Box 2848, Eastbourne, BN20 7XP

1 Father, I thank you with my voice,
    With my voice, with my voice.
    Father, I thank you with my voice,
    With my voice.

2 Father, I thank you with my hands,
    With my hands, with my hands.
    Father, I thank you with my hands,
    With my hands.

3 Father, I thank you with my feet,
    With my feet, with my feet.
    Father, I thank you with my feet,
    With my feet.

4 Father, I thank you with my voice,
    With my hands, with my feet.
    Father, I thank you with my voice,
    Hands and feet.

with my voice –
gently tap upper chest on
each word

with my hands –
clap low on 'with', middle
on 'my', high on 'hands'

with my feet –
stamp on each word

Guidance note:
This is a song for younger children, which explores simple ways to express the joy of being alive – by singing, clapping our hands and stamping our feet.

Story:
Spludge by Steve Stickley

'Spludge come back! Spludge! Stupid dog.' Chris lay on his back in the field. His ankle was broken, he didn't have his mobile, and the dog had run off. And now it was raining. 'Oh no...' Things had gone from bad to worse that day.

Earlier, Chris had to mop up a puddle on the kitchen floor.
'Mum, I'll be late for school,' he'd moaned.
'He's your dog and you clear up his mess!' A scruffy and shaggy Spludge looked at him.
'You're a pain, that's what you are – a pesky mutt!'

After school, mum said 'Take Spludge for a walk before you play with your mates, and then feed him.' So that's how it had happened. Chris hadn't seen the hole – he fell, twisting his ankle right over. He now realised he wouldn't be playing football for some time.

Staring at the darkening clouds, cold, helpless, and near to tears, Chris winced. His ankle was agony.

'Stupid, stupid dog. It's all his fault.' Suddenly Spludge appeared, followed by Chris's mum. 'Good job Spludge loves you,' she said, helping him stand on his good leg. Chris couldn't believe it, Spludge had actually gone home to get help. He was so grateful, even the rain clouds seemed all right now.

© 2003 Steve Stickley, A&C Black Publishers Ltd

Reflection:
Ask the children to think of someone they would like to thank – a parent, carer, teacher or friend – and to sing the song quietly in their heads for that person.

Prayer:
Dear God, we thank you for everything we enjoy. AMEN

5. Shout for joy

Words Psalm 100, music by Peter Readman
© 2003 Note-orious Productions Ltd, A&C Black Publishers Ltd

Chorus
Shout for joy to the Lord!
Shout for joy to the Lord!
Come before him with joyful songs.
Shout for joy to the Lord!

1 Know that the Lord is God and we are his,
     Worship the Lord with all your heart.
   Know that the Lord is God and we are his,
     Worship the Lord with all your heart.
   Chorus

2 Enter his gate with thanks, his courts with praise,
     Give thanks to him and praise his name.
   Enter his gate with thanks, his courts with praise,
     Give thanks to him and praise his name.
   Chorus

3 To all the generations, God is good,
     Praise him for his eternal love.
   To all the generations, God is good,
     Praise him for his eternal love.
   Chorus

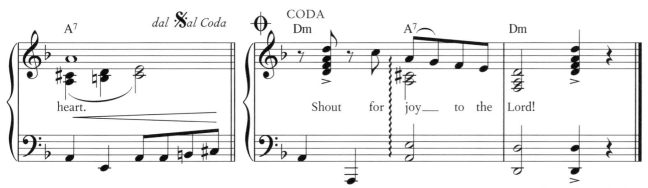

6. Endless Praise

Words from Psalm 8:1, music by David Stoll
© 2003 David Stoll, A&C Black Publishers Ltd

O Lord, our Lord.
   How majestic is your name in all the earth!
You have set your glory on high,
   High above the heavens.
From the lips of children you have asked for praises.
   O Lord, our God and king.

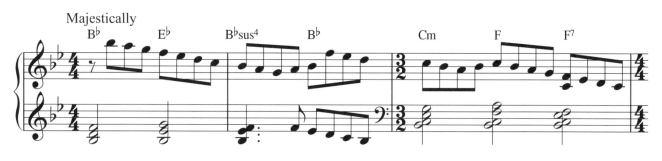

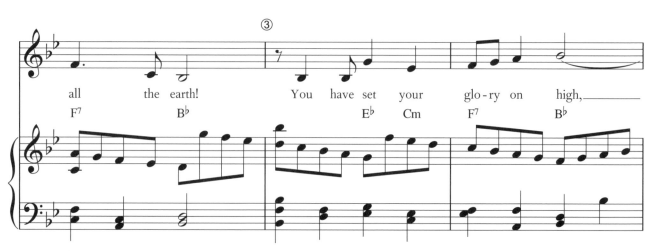

④ High a-bove the hea - vens._ From the lips ⑤ of chil - dren

Eb Cm F7 Bb Eb Cm

⑥ you have asked for prais - es._ O Lord,_ our God and king.

F7 Bb Eb Cm F7 Bb

1.

2. God and king.

Bb F7

Optional Chorus (to start at the 'round' point of entry and continue ad lib
to the end of the piece.)

O Lord, our Lord, O Lord, our Lord.

Guidance note:

This is a setting of part of Psalm 8, in which God is praised. The song
allows for the praise to be 'endless' because it is written as a round, which
may be repeated as many times as required. The numbers 1 – 6 above
the music indicate where each voice part can join in.

Christian talking point:

Ask the children to imagine being part of a global choir of children
singing praises to God in hundreds of different languages. For a class
assembly, translate the words into some of the languages represented in
your school and sing the new verses as a round.

Prayer:

*Dear God, you have asked for praise from children. Please accept this,
our song of praise, and add it to all the songs of praise that are being
sung for you throughout the world. AMEN*

7. Siya hamba

Words and music traditional African
This arrangement © 2003 A&C Black Publishers Ltd

1 Siya hamb' e ku kha nye ni kwen khos,
   Siya hamb' e ku kha nye ni kwen khos.
Siya hamb' e ku kha nye ni kwen khos,
   Siya hamb' e ku kha nye ni kwen khos.
Siya hamba, Oo,
   Siya hamb' e ku kha nye ni kwen khos.
Siya hamba, Oo,
   Siya hamb' e ku kha nye ni kwen khos.

2 We are marching in the light of God,
   We are marching in the light of God.
We are marching in the light of God,
   We are marching in the light of God.
We are marching, Oo,
   We are marching in the light of God.
We are marching , Oo,
   We are marching in the light of God.

3 We are living in the love of God…

4 We are moving in the power of God…

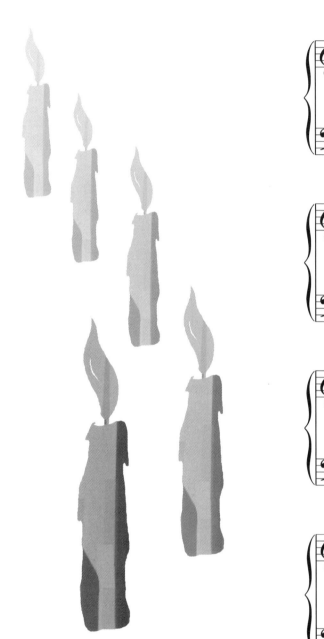

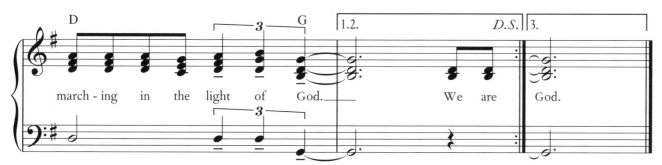

Guidance note:

This song is based on the Bible verse 'Let us walk in the light of the Lord' (Isaiah 2:5) and expresses a desire to live God's way. It is a firm favourite in the repertoire of the African Children's Choir (www.fitw.com) – a choir made up of children from Uganda, Kenya, Rwanda, Nigeria and Ghana, many of whom have suffered due to wars and famine.

Story:

Nkosi *by the Reverend Michael Schaeffer from the Church of England in South Africa (CESA)*

During a summer holiday club, a church in South Africa organised games, songs, good things to eat and Bible stories each day for the children. Nkosi, who was a very poor little boy, heard all the music and laughter and looked through the church window. He saw so many children having fun that he wanted to stay, but he was poor and dirty and didn't know anyone. Just as he was about to walk away, Uncle John who was running the club, saw him and invited him in. For the next few days Nkosi had a wonderful time and especially loved the stories about Jesus. On the second last day, Uncle John asked the children to bring something to give to Jesus to show their love for him. Nkosi went away sadly as he had nothing to give. The next day the children placed their gifts of money, toys, food and clothes on a big tray brought round by Uncle John. Finally Uncle John came to Nkosi.

'Could you bring the tray a little lower, Uncle John?' asked Nkosi. The tray was lowered. 'A little more, Uncle John?' And the tray was lowered further still. 'Could you lower it all the way down, Uncle John?' asked Nkosi.

Uncle John put the tray on the ground. Nkosi climbed onto the tray. 'I will give myself to Jesus,' he said. 'Do you think that will be all right with him, Uncle John?'

'Yes, Nkosi' said Uncle John, 'I think that will suit Jesus just fine.'

General talking point:

African choirs not only sing as one, they also move as one, using simple but effective choreography to accompany their songs. The effect as we watch is of one body marching, living and moving together – an inspiring symbol of community.

Reflection:

Ask the children to consider ways they personally could improve the unity and harmony of their school, class or family.

Prayer:

Dear God, thank you for showing us your ways. Please let us walk in your light, living the way you want us to. AMEN

Words and music traditional, words for verses 2 and 3 by Sue Fearon
This arrangement © 2003 A&C Black Publishers Ltd

1 My God is so big, so strong and so mighty,
   There's nothing that he cannot do.
My God is so big, so strong and so mighty,
   There's nothing that he cannot do.
The rivers are his, the mountains are his,
   The stars are his handiwork too.
My God is so big, so strong and so mighty,
   There's nothing that he cannot do.

2 My God is so big, so strong and so mighty,
   There's nothing that he cannot do.
My God is so big, so strong and so mighty,
   There's nothing that he cannot do.
He brings out the sun, he sends down the rain,
   And makes all the seeds to break through.
My God is so big, so strong and so mighty,
   There's nothing that he cannot do.

3 My God is so big, so strong and so mighty,
   There's nothing that he cannot do.
My God is so big, so strong and so mighty,
   There's nothing that he cannot do.
He gives me his peace, he gives me his love,
   And helps me to love others too.
My God is so big, so strong and so mighty,
   There's nothing that he cannot do.

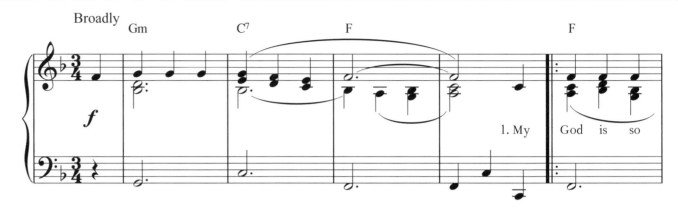

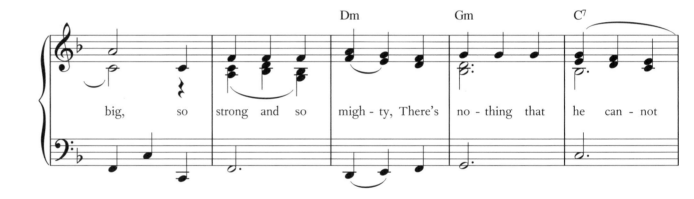

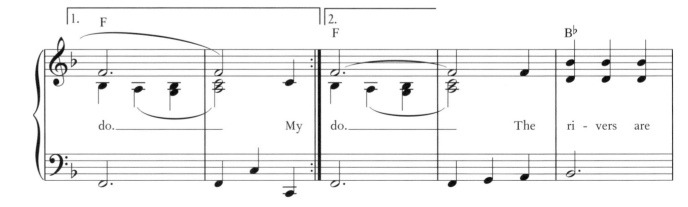

his, the moun-tains are his, The stars are his han-di-work

too. My God is so big, so strong and so

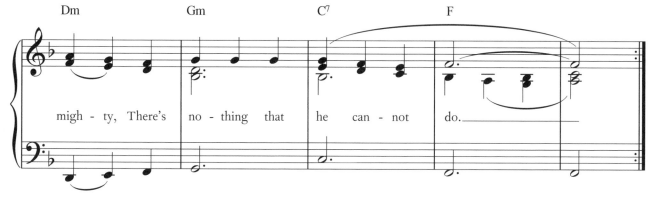

migh-ty, There's no-thing that he can-not do.

Guidance note:
The unlimited power of God is expressed here in a simple action song suitable for all ages.

Bible story (2 Kings 4:1–7):
A woman's husband died owing money and her sons were about to be taken as slaves to clear the debt. The widow appealed to the prophet Elisha, who asked what she had of value. She had nothing but some oil. Oil was used for cooking, medicine and for ceremonial purposes, and was very valuable, but she only had a little. Elisha told her to borrow as many empty jars as she could from her neighbours, then to shut her doors and pour oil from her jar into the ones she had borrowed. The oil kept flowing until all the borrowed jars were full. The woman was able to sell the oil to pay her debts and keep her sons.

Reflection:
Ask the children to think about how they could support and help each other in difficult situations.

Prayer:
Dear God, when we feel powerless and helpless, please remind us that there is nothing that you cannot do. AMEN

big   strong   mighty   nothing

rivers   mountains

stars

9. Danasi

Words and music traditional Ghanaian
This arrangement © 2003 A&C Black Publishers Ltd

Danasi, danasi, da oname asi.
　Danasi, danasi, da oname asi.
Efise oye, na na do doso,
　Danasi, danasi, da oname asi.

Translation
Thank the Lord, thank the Lord, thank the Almighty.
　Thank the Lord, thank the Lord, thank the Almighty.
For he is good and his love shall endure,
　Thank the Lord, thank the Lord, thank the Almighty.

Guidance note:
This Ghanaian praise song is based on the opening verse of Psalms 107, 118 and 136. 'Oh, thank God – he's so good! His love never runs out.'

Prayer:
Dear God, thank you that you are good and that your love will last forever. Please help us to trust in your goodness even in difficult circumstances. AMEN

10. Halle, hallelujah!

Words traditional, music anon
This arrangement © 2003 A&C Block Publishers Ltd

Halle, halle, hallelujah!
   Halle, halle, hallelujah!
Halle, halle, hallelujah!
   Hallelujah, hallelujah! (hallelujah!)

Halle, halle, hallelujah!
   Halle, halle, hallelujah!
Halle, halle, hallelujah!
   Hallelujah, hallelujah! (hallelujah!)

Guidance note:

Hallelujah (or alleluia) means 'praise ye the Lord'. Hallelujah (or alleluia) is a transliteration of a Hebrew liturgical call meaning 'praise you Yahweh'. Yahweh is the covenant name of God rather than a title, such as Lord or Father for example. Hallelujah translates most readily today into a call to praise God. In most schools the use of songs centred on hallelujah or alleluia will be totally acceptable, but in some schools careful consideration should be given as to their appropriateness.

Prayer:

Dear God, you are perfect and good, trustworthy and faithful. Please help us to understand who you are, so that we will praise you more. AMEN

Words and music anon
This arrangement © 2003 A&C Black Publishers Ltd

Alleluia, alleluia.
    Alleluia, alleluia.
Alleluia, alleluia.
    Alleluia, alleluia.

Alleluia, alleluia.
    Alleluia, alleluia.
Alleluia, alleluia.
    Alleluia, alleluia.

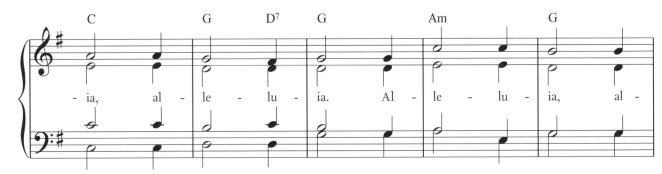

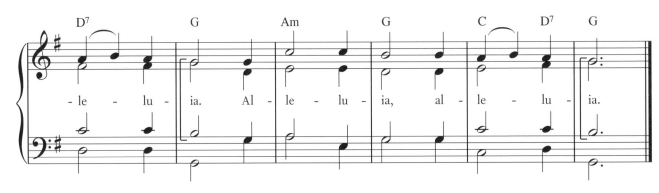

Guidance note:
See note for *Halle, hallelujah.* There are over two hundred calls to 'praise the Lord' in the book of Psalms.

General talking point:
Ask the children to consider how they might evaluate their own talents honestly and how they might recognise and encourage the talents of others through giving praise.

Prayer:
Dear God, please help us to praise you as you deserve. AMEN

12. Our Father in heaven

Words and music by Sheila Wilson
© 1999 Redhead Music Limited, from 'New Millennium Heroes!'

Our Father in heaven:
   We praise your wonderful name!
Your kingdom come, your will be done,
   On earth and heaven the same.
Give us this day our daily bread,
   And forgive us the sins we do and say.
Help us forgive those who've done us wrong,
   And keep us out of evil's way.

For yours is the kingdom!
   Yours the power!
For ever and ever, Amen!
   Yours is the glory!
Yours the praise!
   For ever and ever, Amen!

Yours is the kingdom!
   Yours the power!
For ever and ever, Amen!
   Yours is the glory!
Yours the praise!
   For ever and ever, Amen!

Guidance note:
This song is based on the prayer that Jesus shared with his disciples when they asked how they should pray (Luke 11: 1–4) and is commonly known as the Lord's Prayer. A careful reading of the words will show that it is suitable for use in collective worship in most schools.

Bible story (Matthew 18:23–35):
Adapted by Katherine Kermode

One day a certain king was checking how his servants had managed his money. One servant owed him a great deal of money, about a million pounds, which he was unable to pay back to the king. So the king ordered his guards to take the servant, along with his wife, children and everything they owned, to be sold at the slave market.

The servant threw himself at the king's feet and begged, 'Please, give me a chance and I'll pay it all back'. The king took pity on his servant, forgave him the debt and released him.

A few days later the same servant saw one of his fellow servants who in turn owed him about five pounds. He grabbed him and shouted, 'I want my money. Pay me what you owe.' That servant threw himself down and begged, 'Please be patient with me and I'll pay it all back.' But the first servant wouldn't let him have more time and instead, had him arrested and put into jail until the debt was paid.

When his fellow servants saw what had happened, they were really angry and went and told the king. The king summoned the first servant and said, 'You wicked servant! I forgave you and forgot your debt to me when you begged me to. Couldn't you also have forgiven your fellow servant as I forgave you?' The king was enraged and sent the first servant to prison until he could pay back the sum that he originally owed. The first servant had to stay in prison because he couldn't forgive, although he had been shown great forgiveness himself by the king.

Reflection:

Ask the children to bring to mind someone they'd like to forgive and think kindly of them.

The Lord's Prayer:
Our Father in heaven,
Hallowed be your name,
Your kingdom come,
Your will be done,
On earth as in heaven.
Give us today our daily bread.
Forgive us our sins
As we forgive those who sin against us.
Lead us not into temptation
But deliver us from evil.
For the kingdom, the power,
And the glory are yours
Now and forever. AMEN

13. O Lord, hear my prayer

Words and music by Jacques Berthier
© Ateliers et Presses de Taizé, 71250 Taizé-Community, France

O Lord, hear my prayer,
　O Lord, hear my prayer:
When I call answer me.
　O Lord, hear my prayer,
O Lord, hear my prayer:
　Come and listen to me.

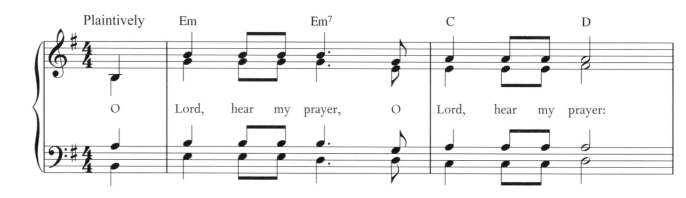

Guidance note:
This is a simple, uncontroversial prayer asking God to respond to the petitioner.

General talking point:
Christians believe that prayer is a very special and privileged communication with God. When a ship is launched, a pair of scissors cuts the ribbon on a bottle of champagne which strikes the ship and launches it. But in reality the ribbon is only a signal for the power of gravity to be released, causing chocks to be removed and restraining chains and cables loosened. Christians show their openness to the release of God's power through prayer.

Reflection:
Ask the children to think about what it must be like to hear every prayer in the world all at once.

Prayer:
Dear God, please help us to remember the extent of your power. And help us to pray wisely. AMEN

14. Be Still and Know

Words and music anon, words for verse 3 by Sue Fearon
This arrangement © 2003 A&C Black Publishers Ltd

1 Be still and know that I am God.
   Be still and know that I am God.
   Be still and know that I am God.

2 By faith alone, God's grace is found.
   By faith alone, God's grace is found.
   By faith alone, God's grace is found.

3 Our faith it is a gift from God.
   Our faith it is a gift from God.
   Our faith it is a gift from God.

4 In you, O Lord, I put my trust.
   In you, O Lord, I put my trust.
   In you, O Lord, I put my trust.

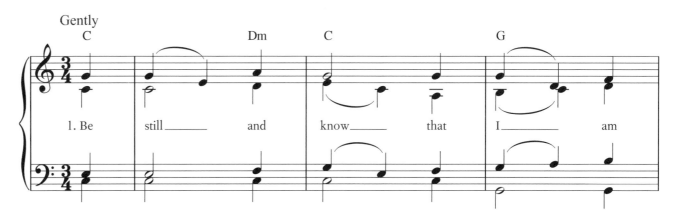
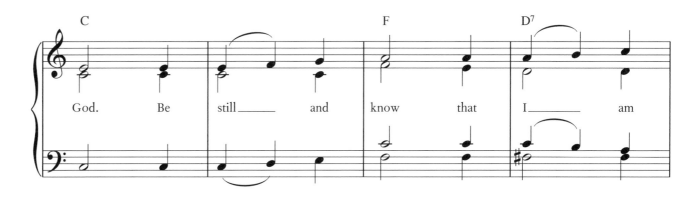
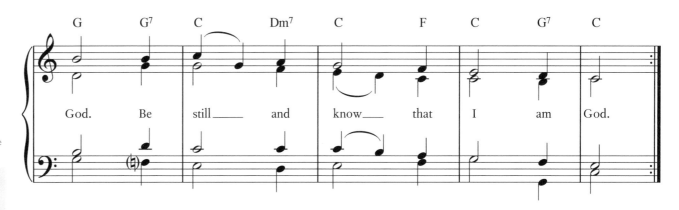

Guidance note:
A reflective song taking its content from Psalm 46:10 and Ephesians 2:8.

Christian talking point:
Christians believe that the faith that we have is a gift from God (Ephesians 2:8). However, faith is a bit like a muscle – the more we practise using the faith we have been given to trust in God, the stronger our faith will become.

Reflection:
Ask each pupil to close their eyes and to be completely still, dismissing any stray thoughts that come into their heads, concentrating only on the words of the song they have sung.

Prayer:
Dear God, please help us to trust you more today than yesterday, and more tomorrow than today. AMEN

Protect me, O Lord, for my boat is so small.
   Protect me, O Lord, for my boat is so small.
My boat is so small and your sea is so wide.
   Protect me, O Lord.

Protect me, O Lord, for my boat is so small.
   Protect me, O Lord, for my boat is so small.
My boat is so small and your sea is so wide.
   Protect me, O Lord.

Guidance note:
This can be sung as a partner song to *Safe with the Lord*. Try singing no 15 once, then no 16 once, then both together.

Christian talking point:
People can sometimes seem small and insignificant. A boat on the horizon can be hard to pick out from the shore and crowds of people seen from the top of a tall building look like ants. In Psalm 8, you can read how King David marvelled that God had time for and cared about individual people.

Reflection:
Ask the children to think how they might help someone who feels scared and unimportant.

Prayer:
Dear God, we know that your world can sometimes be a big and dangerous place. Please help us to trust in you for our safety and protection. AMEN

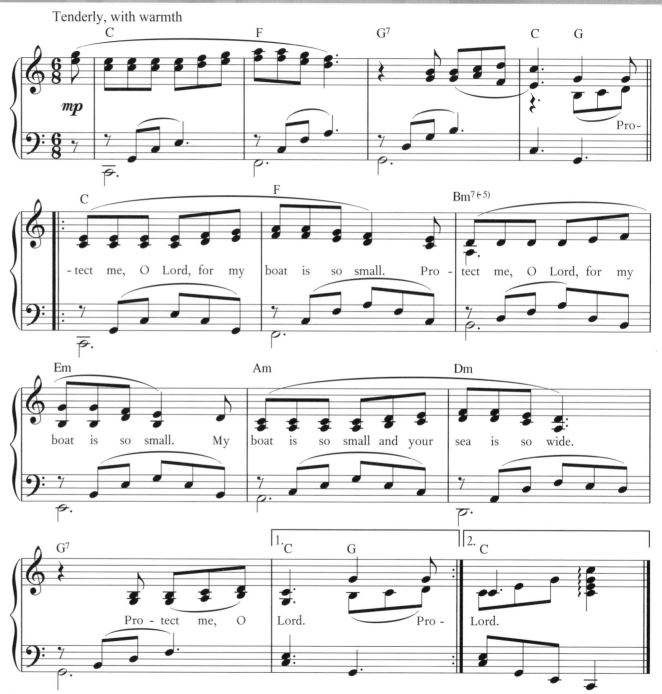

16. safe with the Lord

Words and music by Dot Fraser
© 2003 Dot Fraser, A&C Black Publishers Ltd

Safe on the high seas,
    Safe on the calm seas.
Over the wide seas,
    Safe, safe with the Lord.

Safe on the high seas,
    Safe on the calm seas.
Over the wide seas,
    Safe, safe with the Lord.

Guidance note:
Christians find their safety in Jesus; however the term Lord in this song may be interpreted as simply the Lord God which would make it acceptable to a wider range of children. This song can be sung as a partner song to the *Breton fisherman's prayer*.

When the storm rose *by Carla Moss*
(Sounds: rainmakers, whistles and siren whistles, wobble boards)

Jesus and his friends were out at sea   *(tap two fingers on palms)*
In a big wooden boat on Galilee.
Jesus was asleep when the rain started pouring   *(tapping gets louder)*
The waves got higher but he kept snoring
When the storm rose up on the sea of Galilee.   *(drum on knees)*

'Help!' cried the men, 'we're all gonna drown!'   *(drumming gets louder)*
Disturbed from his sleep, Jesus woke with a frown.
'Chill, don't worry, you'll come to no harm'.
And he said to the wind and the waves, 'Be calm',   *(drumming stops)*
When the storm rose up on the sea of Galilee.

The friends looked at Jesus, stunned and amazed,   *(rub hands together*
But Jesus was Jesus and quite unfazed.   *to sound like water*
Who is this man who gave the word   *lapping against*
That the wind and the rain and the waves all heard,   *the boat)*
When the storm rose up on the sea of Galilee?

© 2003 Carla Moss, A&C Black Publishers Ltd

Reflection:
Ask the children to spend some time thinking about the people who risk their lives at sea and the comfort this song might be to them.

Prayer:
Lord, please help us to understand what it means to be safe with you.
Help us to trust you even when things are not going well for us. AMEN

Words and music by Julia Wagstaff
© 2003 Julia Wagstaff, A&C Black Publishers Ltd

1 Lord God when all our dreams seem changed
     And all is far from sure,
   Help us to trust your loving care
     To keep us safe and secure.

2 Lord God, when friendships fall apart
     And we feel left behind,
   Help us to trust in you, O Lord,
     For you are faithful and kind.

3 Lord God, when we in fear step out,
     Find it hard to see the way,
   We know, dear Lord, your light will shine
     And lead us on into day.

Optional verse for times of tragedy
4 When sadness tears our lives apart,
     All seems to be in vain,
   Your joy will come to us, O Lord,
     And lead us on again.

5 Thank you for all the ways you lead,
     And for your loving plan,
   Help us to listen, Lord, to you
     And ever hold your hand.

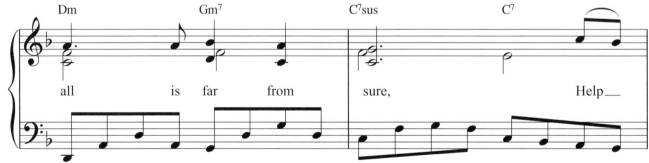

us   to trust   your   lov - ing   care   To___

1.2.3.4.

5. rit.

keep   us   safe   and   se - cure._____ 2.Lord___   hand.

18. In the light

Words and music by Susannah Pearse
© 2003 Susannah Pearse, A&C Black Publishers Ltd

1 When it's dark, late at night
   And you can't get to sleep
'Cause you're sure there's a monster
   Getting ready to leap,
You can't see it clearly
   But you know that it's there;
Might be a dragon or a bear!

Throw some light on the question
   And the answer is clear,
It is only a jumper
   On the back of a chair.
There aren't any monsters
   So there's nothing to fear,
No sign of dragons or of bears.

Chorus
In the light,
   Everything is clearer.
In the light
   Shadows disappear.
In the light
   You can see what's really there,
Never mind what's nearly there,
   See clearly in the light.

2 When it's dark, late at night
   And a ship sails for shore,
Though the harbour approaches
   There are dangers in store.
The boat can be caught
   By jagged rocks that are there.
Captain! It's best that you beware!

light on the ques-tion And the an-swer is clear,___ It is on-ly a jum-per On the

back of a chair.___ There aren't a-ny mon-sters So there's no-thing to fear,___

No sign of dra-gons or of bears. In the light_____

Shine a light on the water
    And the way becomes clear,
Now the ship cannot falter
    So there's nothing to fear.
The lighthouse can shine a beam
    To bring the boat in,
Safely the journey can begin.

Chorus
Shine a light...
    ...See clearly in the light.

3 If your world is in darkness
    And you struggle to smile,
And you're feeling unhappy
    And have been for a while,
You can't find a way
    To make it through on your own,
You're stuck in the darkness all alone.

Seek a light in the dark
    To make your way become clear,
Seek a light in the dark
    To take away all your fear,
The light of the world is there just waiting to shine,
    He'll shine in your life and in mine.

Chorus
Shine a light...
    ...See clearly in the light.

In the light!

really there,_____ Never mind what's nearly there, See

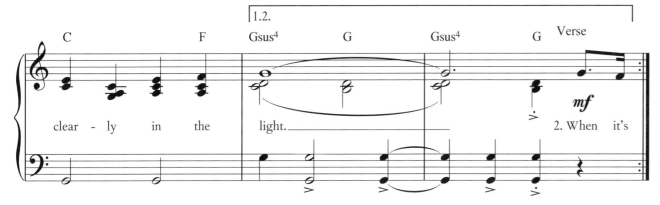

clearly in the light._____ 2. When it's

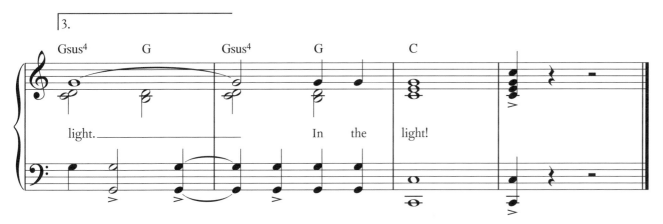

light._____ In the light!

19. one more to count

Words and music by Eileen and Alan Simmons
© 2001 Alan Simmons Music, PO Box 7, Scissett, Huddersfield HD8 9YZ

1 You were born in times of trouble,
   In a strange, unfriendly place,
Where a father's strength and wisdom
   And a mother's warmth and grace
Kept you there, all meek and gentle,
   As their cares began to mount,
And to them you were a saviour,
   But to others you were just one more to count.

But when you came you taught compassion,
   You taught us how we must forgive,
And we listened
   As you taught us how to live.

2 From a vain and cruel ruler
   To survive you had to flee
From your home and from your country,
   Just another refugee;
You were in the hands of strangers
   In an unfamiliar place,
Were you welcomed and accepted?
   Did they help you with your unfamiliar face?

Or were there those whose loud complaining
   Would send you back the way you came?
Was it different?
   Is the world today the same?

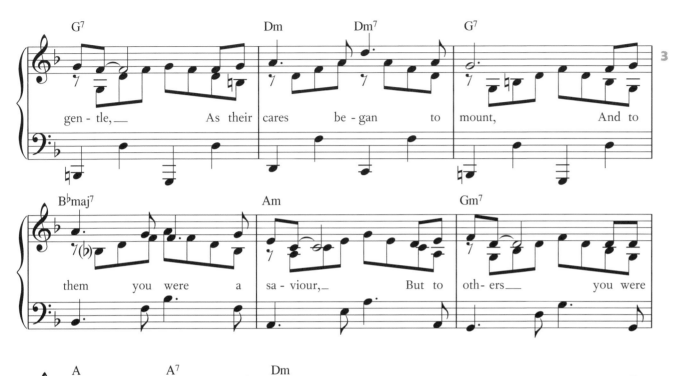

gen - tle,___ As their cares be - gan to mount, And to

them you were a sa - viour,___ But to oth- ers___ you were

just one more to count. But when you

came you taught com - pas - sion,___ You taught us how we must for -

3 Through the years your life has echoed,
   Every deed and every word
 Given hope to many people,
   As your message has been heard,
 Ah, but are your words still heeded?
   By their strength we stand or fall,
 As we look around the planet
   Did we listen? Did we really hear at all?

 For when you came you taught compassion,
   You taught us that we must forgive,
 Did we listen?
   Did we really learn to live?

20. The man from Galilee

Words by Sue Fearon, music traditional
© 2003 Sue Fearon , A&C Black Publishers Ltd

1 The man from Galilee spoke to the people,
   They crowded round to hear his words so simple.
His message was so clear but hard to honour,
   He called upon them all to love their neighbour.

2 The man from Galilee told many stories,
   He told of one left ill because of robbers.
The priest and scribe passed by without a murmur,
   The enemy it was who loved his neighbour.

3 The man from Galilee said to the people,
   'For those who'd follow me my rules are simple.
Just love the Lord your God with mind and labour,
   And do the best you can to love your neighbour.'

4 The man from Galilee, through Scripture's pages,
   Speaks to a child like me across the ages.
I know that I should care for friend and stranger.
   So I will try today to love my neighbour.

Guidance note:
This song represents Jesus as a historical figure and looks at the story of the good samaritan. (Luke 10: 25 – 37)

Prayer:
Dear God, please help us to see everyone in the way that you see them, and show us how to love and help anyone in need. AMEN

Words by Christina Lane, music traditional
Words © 2003 Christina Lane , A&C Black Publishers Ltd

1 Vroom! Vroom! Goes the pizza delivery man,
Delivery man, delivery man,
Vroom! Vroom! Goes the pizza delivery man,
And his most magnificent pizza.

2 The ears of wheat grew high in the field...

3 The tomatoes grew in a big, glass house...

4 The mushrooms grew in a cold, dark cave...

5 The olives were picked and pickled in a jar...

6 The peppers sailed in a crate on a ship...

7 The pineapples flew on a supersonic jet...

8 The grated cheese was sprinkled on the top...

9 We thank you God, for the foods you give..
...For the most magnificent pizza.

Guidance note:
A fun harvest song which can be sung as a partner song to
Harvest thanks.

General talking point:
For a class assembly, link pictures of pizza ingredients to a map showing
their country of origin. Consider the many people who have had a hand
in making the pizza by planting, watering, reaping, milking, chopping, or
packaging the ingredients.

Tip:
Visit www.oxfam.org.uk/fair_trade.html

Prayer:
*Dear God, thank you for all the good things that you give us. Thank you
for our food and for all those who have a part in providing it for us.*
AMEN

Words by Christina Lane, music traditional
Words © 2003 Christina Lane , A&C Black Publishers Ltd

1 Soon as we all reap crops for harvest,
 Crops for harvest, crops for harvest,
 Soon as we all reap crops for harvest
 We give thanks to God.

2 Soon as we all reap wheat for flour…

3 Soon as we all pick red tomatoes…

4 Soon as we all pick button mushrooms…

5 Soon as we all pick juicy olives…

6 Soon as we all pick crunchy peppers…

7 Soon as we all pick big pineapples…

8 Soon as we all make tasty cheeses…

9 Soon as we all eat what we harvest...

 …We give thanks to God.

Guidance note:
This song may be sung as a partner song to *The most magnificent pizza.*

Assembly suggestion:
Many Christians make it a practise to say grace – thank you to God –
before eating. Collect from the children, their parents and the wider
community some examples of prayers of thanksgiving from a variety of
cultures and faiths to share at an assembly.

Prayer:
The Selkirk Grace (an old Scottish prayer of thanks)

Some hae meat and canna eat, (Some have food but cannot eat it)
And some wad eat that want it; (Some have no food)
But we hae meat, and we can eat, (We have food and can eat)
And sae the Lord be thankit. (So thank you, Lord.)

23. Like a candle flame

Words and music by Graham Kendrick
© 1988 Make Way Music, PO Box 263, Croydon, CR9 5AP, UK

1 Like a candle flame,
   Flick'ring small in our darkness.
   Uncreated light shines through infant eyes.
      God is with us, alleluia,
   Come to save us, alleluia, allelulia!

2 Stars and angels sing,
   Yet the earth sleeps in the shadows;
   Can this tiny spark set a world on fire?
      God is with us, alleluia,
   Come to save us, alleluia, allelulia!

3 Yet his light shall shine
   From our lives, spirit blazing,
   As we touch the flame of his holy fire.
      God is with us, alleluia,
   Come to save us, alleluia, allelulia!

      God is with us, alleluia,
   Come to save us, alleluia, allelulia!

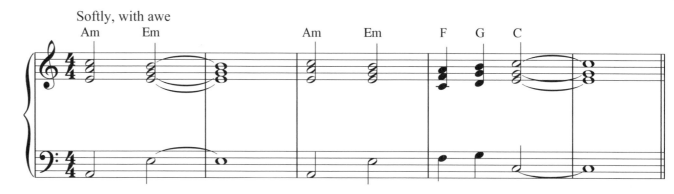

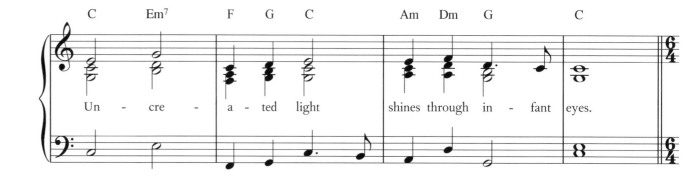

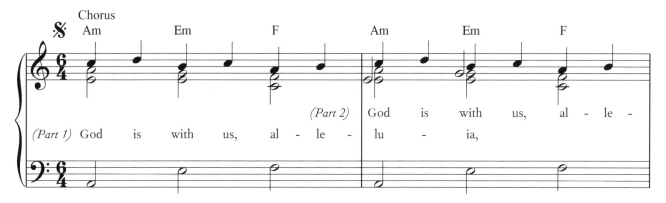

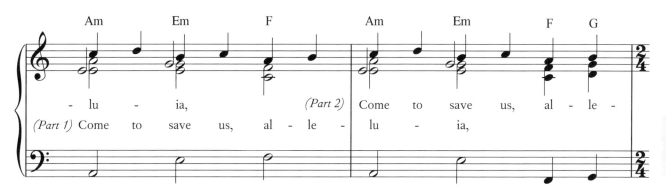

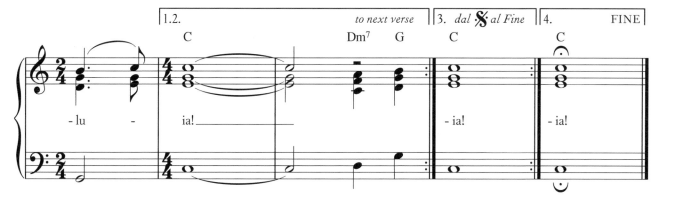

Guidance note:
This song uses poetic language to describe the Christian belief in the incarnation. Careful consideration should be given to the way in which this song is used in a school with pupils from a variety of faith backgrounds. A good approach is to remind pupils that they are not required to sing anything that they, or their parents, would not be happy about.

Talking point:
The song draws on the metaphor that Jesus is the light of the world which is explained alongside *In the light*. In this song, Jesus is compared to a small candle flame to describe the way he entered the world, not as its creator, but as a baby (John 1:1-18). Christians believe that Jesus, as part of the Godhead (that is, the Father, Son and Holy Spirit) was instrumental in creation, yet chose to enter into the world as a helpless baby. Using a cake with birthday candles, ask the children to tell you in which year they were born. Light the candles, explaining that our calendar is based on the year that Jesus was born. So those born in the year 2000 were born two thousand years after Jesus.

Reflection:
Light a candle and ask the children to reflect upon what they know about Jesus.

Prayer:
Dear God, please help us to understand what happened that first Christmas. Help each one of us to understand who Jesus is and how we should respond to him. AMEN

Words and music by Sheila Wilson
© 2003 Sheila Wilson, Redhead Music Ltd, A&C Black Publishers Ltd

We come to you, Lord,
   Like the wise men of old.
We long to bring gifts
   As the wise men brought gold.
But we have no treasure,
   No jewels, or crown;
We simply come to you
   And lay our hearts down.

We sing 'Hallelujah, Hallelu'
   Hallelujah, we love you.
Hallelujah, Hallelu'
   Hallelujah, we love you'.

Everyone's singing, Lord • © 2003 A&C Black Publishers Ltd • Photocopying without a licence is illegal, see inside front cover

Guidance note:
Very careful consideration should be given in a school with pupils from a variety of faith backgrounds to the way in which this song is used. It is a song of worship to Jesus and may be considered blasphemous by some pupils and their families.

Christian talking point:
Ask the children to imagine going home with a gift which is given to a parent or carer, and that the gift is then ignored. All evening one job after the other needs doing: supper to be cooked, baby to bath, washing up doesn't do itself. Eventually the child goes to bed and the gift is still unopened where it was casually placed. How would they feel? Christians believe that Jesus is God's perfect gift to the whole world (John 3:16). When we get tied up in the razzmatazz of Christmas and don't even think about Jesus, how must God feel?

Talking point:
Many children are taught that three kings bearing gifts arrived at the stable in Bethlehem on Christmas night. Yet, in the Bible account of the visit (Matthew 2:1-12) the men are referred to as Magi, a term meaning wise men or astrologers. No reference is made to their number and the Bible says that they delivered their gifts to a house some time after the birth. Encourage the children to read religious stories directly from Holy books whenever possible, even if the language might be a little difficult.

Reflection:
The wise men must have given up a great deal to make this journey. Ask the children to reflect on someone who is very special to them and for whom they would make a very special effort.

Prayer:
Dear God, please help us to understand the true meaning of Christmas. Help us to think about the perfect gift you gave us in Jesus. AMEN

25. He doesn't look like a king

Words and music by Susannah Pearse
© 2003 Susannah Pearse , A&C Black Publishers Ltd

1 People gather in crowds on the streets
   Waiting for their king.
They have heard of the power he has
   And the triumph he will bring.
But the man that they can see
   Isn't quite what they expect.

Chorus A
He doesn't look like a king,
   He doesn't dress like a king,
He doesn't wear any crown,
   He cannot be our king.
He wears no robes of a king,
   He has no armies with him,
No chariot he brings,
   He cannot be our king,
No, he cannot be our king.

2 Then a voice in the crowd says
   'Careful what you say,
For it says in the prophecies
   That this will be the way,
For our true king comes in peace
   And our true king comes to serve.'

Chorus B
For if he looked like a king,
   If he were dressed like a king,
If he were wearing a crown,
   He could not be our king.
If he wore robes like a king,
   If he had armies with him
Or chariots to bring,
   He could not be our king,
No, he would not be our king.

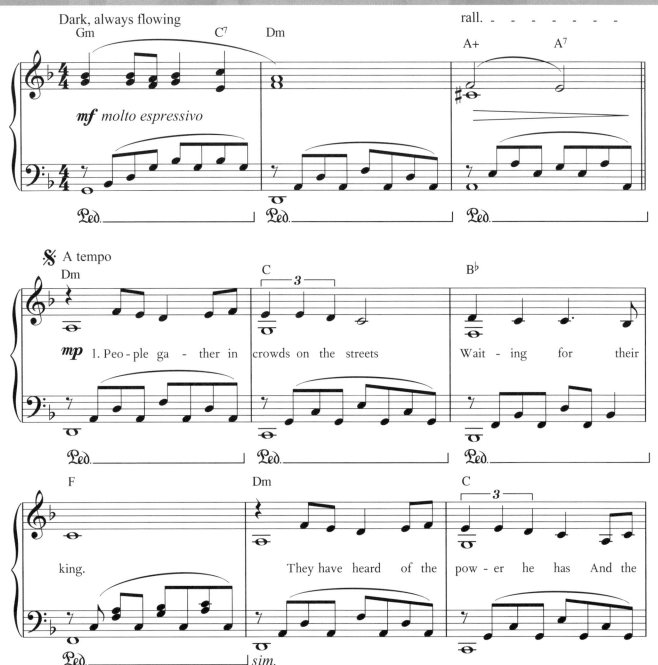

tri - umph he will bring. But the man that

they can see ____ Is - n't quite what

they ex - pect. ____ He does - n't look like a king, ____

3 So they cheer and they shout for him
Arms raised to the sky.
People lay palm leaves down for him
As he's riding by.
And although he comes in peace
They all hail the servant king.
Chorus B

4 'Sing Hosanna!' to the king
Is their welcome cry,
But before the week is out
It turns to 'Crucify!'
For they all will turn from him,
And will say he has to die.
Chorus A

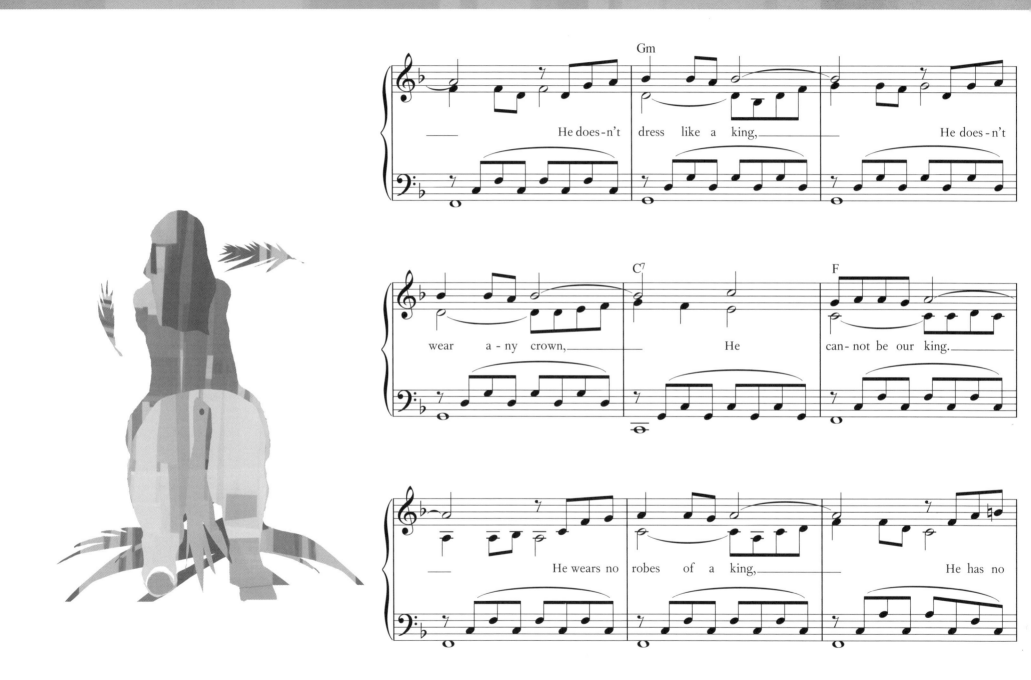

ar - mies with him,____ No cha - ri - ot he brings,____ He

can - not be our king, No, he___ can - not be our king.

can - not be our king.____

Guidance note:
The way in which this song tells the story of Palm Sunday should make it suitable for use in most schools.

Christian talking point:
With Israel being occupied by the Romans, the Jews were desperate for the Messiah to come and save them. (Messiah is the Hebrew word meaning 'God's anointed one' or 'God's chosen king'.) They were expecting a warrior king, someone very like the famous King David. It was being said that Jesus had been healing the lame, giving sight to the blind and even giving new life to the dead. The people of Jerusalem began to believe that Jesus could be the one they had been waiting for. So, on the day he entered Jerusalem to celebrate the Jewish Passover feast the people lined the streets, cheered him and laid palm leaves at his feet (John 12:12-15). Imagine their thoughts when Jesus passed by on a donkey's colt. Was this truly the promised Messiah? How would the children expect a great king to arrive?

Prayer:
Dear God, please help us to see things your way. When we want to fight, show us ways of resolving our differences peacefully. AMEN

26. For God so loved the world

Words and music by John Hardwick
© 1992 Daybreak Music Ltd, PO Box 2848, Eastbourne, BN20 7XP

For God so loved the world
 He gave his only son,
And whoever believes in him
 Shall not die, but have eternal life.

L is for the love that he has for me,
I am the reason he died on the tree.
F is for forgiveness and now I am free,
E is to enjoy being in his company.

For God so loved the world
 He gave his only son,
And whoever believes in him
 Shall not die, but have eternal life.

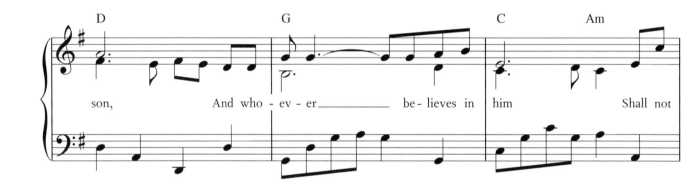

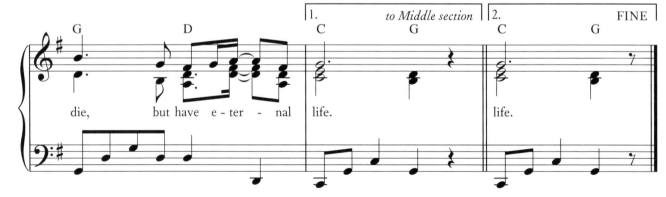

N.B. The two sections can be sung together

Middle section

'L' is for the love that he has for me, ___

'I' am the rea-son he died on the tree. ___ 'F' is for for-give-ness and

D.C. al Fine

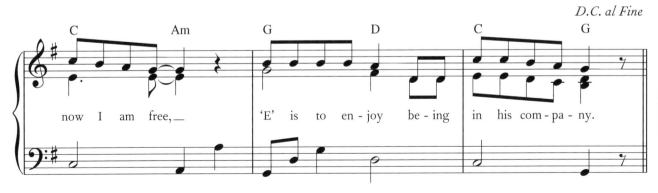

now I am free, ___ 'E' is to en-joy be-ing in his com-pa-ny.

Guidance note:

This song is a setting of John 3:16. It talks about the reason Jesus came to earth – for God to be reunited with people, so that they could be with him, and he with them forever. Some consideration should be given to the way in which this song is used in a school with pupils from a variety of faith backgrounds. A good approach is to remind pupils that they are not required to sing anything that they or their parents would not be happy about.

Story:

The sparrow, the cockerel, the crow and the dove *by Steve Stickley*

Four birds sat in a fig tree in old Palestine. They were having an argument about who was the most important. The squawking was almost deafening.

'It's obvious that I am important because Jesus said so!' chirped the sparrow. 'He said that God is sad every time a sparrow falls to the ground.'

'I am the most important,' strutted the cockerel, 'because when I crowed, I reminded a friend of Jesus that he had done wrong and he was very sorry.'

'Death's important because it comes to us all' cawed the crow. 'I saw him die on the cross and I guarded his grave through the dark night. I'm most important!'

The dove flapped her white wings. 'But I was there when he rose back up from death, when he came alive again. I'm the most important!' And so their arguments continued all day long.

After they had eventually quietened down, a tired voice came from underneath the tree. It was a donkey.

'Call me stupid... call me slow... But I carried Jesus and I saw how the crowds of people loved him. Old and young, big and small, healthy and sick, rich and poor. Maybe we're all as important as each other...'

Reflection:

Ask the children to think about sacrifice; giving up something precious for someone else. Is it an easy thing to do? Why would someone do it?

Prayer:

Dear God, thank you for loving us. Please help us to understand what Jesus did that first Easter. AMEN

Words and music by Ruth Wills
© 1994 Saltmine

1 God is with me now,
   He sees and hears me.
He's smiling down on me
   Because he loves me.

Chorus
God loves me,
   God loves me.
God loves me,
   Now and forever.

2 God is with me now,
   He understands me.
He knows my deepest thoughts,
   Because he loves me.

Chorus
God loves me,
   God loves me.
God loves me,
   Now and forever.

Guidance note:
This song expresses the idea of God's continual presence and loving care.

Christian talking point:
Loneliness can be the most painful of all emotions. Loneliness is not simply experienced by quiet people who are often alone, but also by outgoing people. The Bible states that Jesus said, 'And surely I am with you always, to the very end of the age.' (Matthew 28:20) Explain to the children the Christian belief that Jesus will always be with his people in this world and the next.

Story:
Bella's Lunch by *Steve Stickley*

Everything had gone wrong that morning. Bella couldn't find one of her shoes and had come to school in her dirty trainers. Worse still, she'd forgotten her packed lunch. Bella sat in assembly worrying. It looked like being a dreadful day and worse still, in the first lesson she had to sit next to Ruben. Nobody liked Ruben – he was often in trouble because he sometimes stole other people's things. But Ruben seemed quiet today so Bella ignored him.

By playtime her tummy was rumbling. Everyone else had snacks and Bella pretended that she wasn't hungry. Next lesson, she caught Ruben rummaging through her bag.
'Hey! Get off! What are you doing?'
'Got any chocolate biscuits?' grunted Ruben cheekily. Bella couldn't help it – she cried. She didn't want to, but she cried. She could see that Ruben didn't know what to do, so she told him about forgetting her food and then dried her tears before their teacher noticed.

At dinner time, Ruben came up to her and gave her a sandwich. Bella was amazed! Ruben said nothing. Later, he gave her a banana. When Bella went home that day she thought about Ruben differently. Maybe he wasn't all that bad...

Reflection:
Encourage the children to reflect on one of their friendships and to consider what makes it good.

Prayer:
Dear God, thank you for our friends. Please help us be good friends to one another, particularly those who are alone or hurt. AMEN

28. Father God, you love me

Words and music by Paul Crouch and David Mudie
© 1993 Daybreak Music Ltd, PO Box 2848, Eastbourne BN20 7XP

1 Father God, you love me and
   You know me inside out,
You know the words that I will say
   Before I speak them out.
You are all around me,
   You hold me in your hand.
Your love for me is more than I
   Can ever understand.

2 Father God, from your love
   There is nowhere I can hide.
If I go down into the depths
   Or cross the ocean wide,
There your love would find me,
   You'd take me in your hand.
Your love for me is more
   Than I can ever understand.

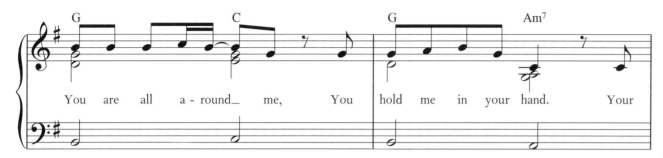

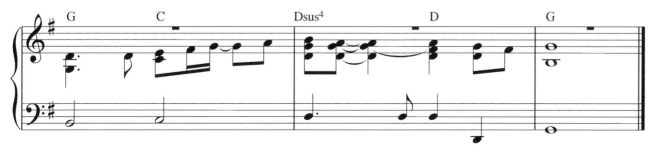

Guidance note:
A song of comfort drawn from the belief that God is everywhere and knows us intimately.

Christian talking point:
When we're little we often have to hold an adult's hand to cross the road. Even if we wanted to let go we couldn't because the adult holds us tightly to keep us safe. Christians believe that God keeps us safe in the same way, because he loves us. (John 10:29)

Prayer:
Dear God, thank you for holding us in your love. Please help us to grow in confidence of your love and care for us, day by day. AMEN

29. I love the pit, pit, patter

Words and music traditional, words of verses 2 and 3 by Sue Fearon
This arrangement © 2003 A&C Black Publishers Ltd

1 I love the pit, pit, patter of the rain-drops,
  I love the buzz, buzz, buzzing of the bees,
  But the thing I love the best, the very, very best,
  Is to know that God loves me.

2 I love the hop, hop, hopping of the robin,
  I love the snow which falls upon the trees,
  But the thing I love the best, the very, very best,
  Is to know that God loves me.

3 I love the splash, splash, splashing of the seaside,
  I love the waves which rise up to my knees,
  But the thing I love the best, the very, very best,
  Is to know that God loves me.

Guidance note:
A song of God's love.

General talking point:
For a class assembly, make a collection of things that bring the children pleasure. The collection might include objects, paintings, poems and prose. Share the lyrics of 'My favourite things' from the musical *The Sound of Music* with the children, and discuss ways in which they could use their favourite things to help them get through more difficult times.

Prayer:
Dear God, thank you that your love is constant and unchanging, and that we can be sure of your love whatever is going on in our lives. AMEN

30. Just a tiny seed

Words and music by Tracey Atkins, Richard Atkins and Andrew Pratt
© 1995 Stainer & Bell Ltd, London, England and The Trustees for Methodist Church Purposes

1 Just a tiny seed,
　　In the earth it goes,
Just a little rain,
　　It begins to grow.

2 From that tiny seed
　　Grows a mighty tree,
Branches spread out wide
　　Shelter you and me.

3 In that mighty tree
　　Birds will perch and sing.
Like the tree, God's love
　　From small seeds can spring.

Guidance note:
This song likens the way in which God's love grows inside us to the way a tiny seed grows into a tree. In one of the parables, Jesus described the kingdom of God as a tiny seed that becomes a mighty tree (Mark 4:30-32).

Reflection:
Ask the children to imagine a 'seed' that they can plant to make their class, school or home a happier place. What would be their favourite seed? eg patience, kindness, friendliness, helpfulness...

Prayer:
Dear God, thank you that your love can grow inside us. Please help us to be more loving to other people. AMEN

31. Nobody's a Nobody

Words and music by John Hardwick
© 1993 Daybreak Music Ltd, PO Box 2848, Eastbourne, BN20 7XP

1 Nobody's a nobody
　 Believe me 'cos it's true.
Nobody's a nobody,
　 Especially not you.
Nobody's a nobody
　 And God wants us to see
That everybody's somebody
　 And that means even me.

2 I'm no cartoon, I'm human,
　 I have feelings, treat me right.
I'm not a superhero
　 With super strength and might.
I'm not a mega pop star
　 Or super athlete,
But did you know I'm special,
　 In fact I'm quite unique.

3 Nobody's a nobody
　 Believe me 'cos it's true.
Nobody's a nobody,
　 Especially not you.
Nobody's a nobody
　 And God wants us to see
That everybody's somebody
　 And that means even me.

feel - ings, treat me right. I'm not a su - per he - ro With

su - per strength_ and might. I'm not a me - ga pop star, Or

su - per a - the - lete, But did you know I'm spe - cial, In

dal %al Coda CODA

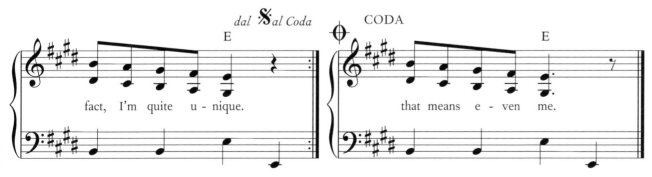

fact, I'm quite u - nique.   that means e - ven me.

Guidance note:
This song deals with one of the key human needs – significance.

Christian talking point:
The Bible says that Jesus treated everyone equally. In one story (John 4:4-28) Jesus speaks kindly to a person treated badly by everybody else. Encourage the children to speak kindly to everyone. If they are being treated as a nobody, remind them that to God they are always somebody.

General talking point:
Creation is full of variety and uniqueness. Ask the children to look around them at others in the school. How much effort would it take to know every one of their fellow students really well? Do they know everyone's name? Suggest that they make a point of speaking to someone they don't know today and every day for a week.

Prayer:
Dear God, thank you for loving each one of us individually. Please help us to love others the way you love us. AMEN

32. Special

Words and music by Paul Field
© 1991 Daybreak Music Ltd, PO Box 2848, Eastbourne, BN20 7XP

There is no-one else like you,
    There's no-one else like me.
Each of us is special to God,
    That's the way it's meant to be.
I'm special, you're special,
    We're special don't you see?
There is no-one else like you,
    There's no-one else like me.

Black or white, short or tall,
    Good or bad, God loves us all.
Loud or quiet, fat or thin,
    Each of us is special to him.

There is no-one else like you,
    There's no-one else like me.
Each of us is special to God,
    That's the way it's meant to be.
I'm special, you're special,
    We're special don't you see?
There is no-one else like you,
    There's no-one else like me.

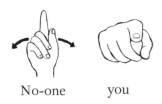

No-one   you

me   special

Everyone's singing, Lord • © 2003 A&C Black Publishers Ltd • Photocopying without a licence is illegal, see inside front cover

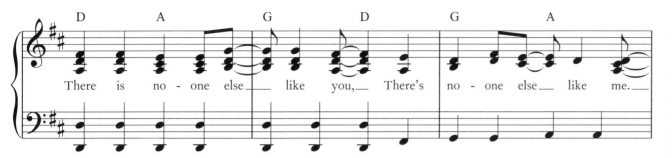

There is no-one else like you, There's no-one else like me.

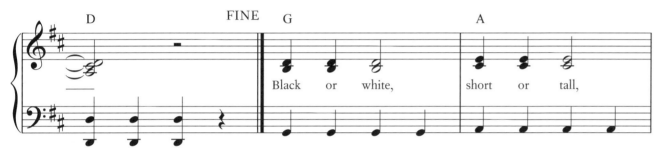

FINE

Black or white, short or tall,

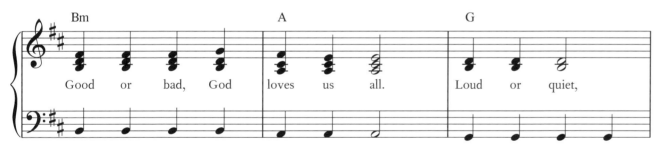

Good or bad, God loves us all. Loud or quiet,

D.C. al Fine

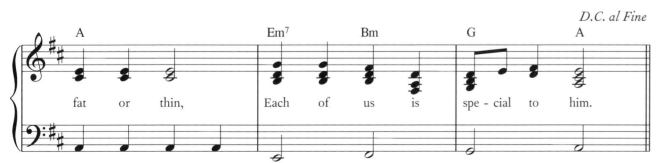

fat or thin, Each of us is spe-cial to him.

Guidance note:
This song deals with the Christian belief that God's love cannot be restricted by man-made rules or ideas, and that we are all special and unique to him.

Story:
Small *adapted from Luke 15: 1–7, by Carla Moss*:

My name's Small. I'm the smallest lamb in our flock, and when you're small it's sometimes easy to get lost. And I did, last week. It was awful. I was so scared. We'd all been up on the hill outside Jerusalem, eating grass as usual, when I saw a really, really tasty plant further down the hill. I had some last week and it was yummy – juicy green leaves and big yellow flowers that taste like honey.

So I went off for a nibble. I wasn't there very long, but when I turned round the others were gone. They'd all disappeared, even Big J too. (Big J's our shepherd, and he is big!) Anyway, I was all alone and there was no Big J, no Mam, no-one. And I cried... Well, I started moving in the direction that I thought they might have gone and I must have walked for miles. It started to get dark and I was even more scared. Mam always says 'don't ever stay out at night because it's not safe'. I didn't believe her before, but I do now. There were so many strange noises and shadows that weren't there in the daytime. And... well... I cried some more. But then I heard Big J shouting 'Small, Small' and I baa-ed and baa-ed. For a moment I thought he might be angry with me, but he rushed up and picked me up and suddenly I felt so safe.

Big J and I went back to the others. Mam told me off, but I know it's only because she loves me and was worried about me.
But, I've learnt my lesson. I'm not wandering off for any more nice yellow flowers, however juicy they look!

© 2003 Carla Moss, A&C Block Publishers Ltd

General talking point:
What does it mean to be special? Discuss the different characters in the story. Get the children to tell the story from Big J and Mam's point of view. What were they feeling?

Reflection:
Think of someone who is special to you. Think of a way you can tell them or show them that they are special.

Prayer:
Dear God, we are all very special to you. Please help us to remember this. And please help us to show other people how special they are to us.
AMEN

33. The Senses Song

Words and music by Ruth Wills and Phil Brown
© 1994 Saltmine

I can hear with my ears, I can smell with my nose,
  I can jump up and down and touch my toes.
I can sing with my mouth that God gave me,
  'Cos my father in heaven made me.

I can sniff, (*sniff, sniff*)
  I can taste, (*bleh*)
I can even talk to him. (*Hi God*)
  I can see your face smiling back at me,
'Cos my father in heaven made me.

I can hear with my ears, I can smell with my nose,
  I can jump up and down and touch my toes.
I can sing with my mouth that God gave me,
  'Cos my father in heaven made me.

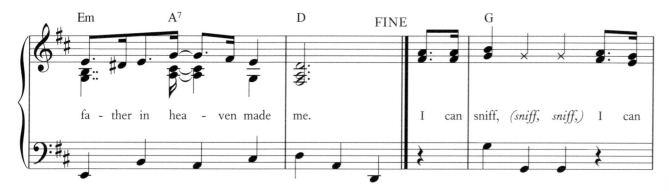

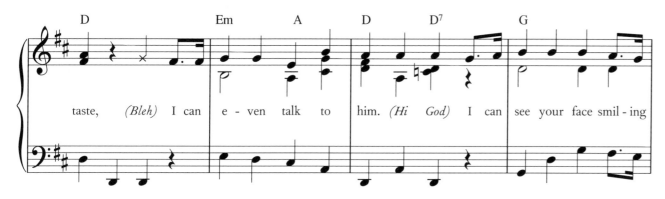

Guidance note:
The lyrics of this song assume a range of physical abilities that may not always be present in every pupil in a school. You may wish to discuss the introduction of this particular song to the school repertoire with colleagues.

Story:
Rich by Carla Moss

Rich is a wheelchair user. He visits schools to talk to children about what life is like using a wheelchair. 'Some people call me disabled, but I say I am a wheelchair user with a disability. I use the wheelchair to get around because I'm unable to walk. This means that shoes last forever, I never get sore feet from too much walking, and you should see me going down hill!'

The children want to know the answer to all sorts of questions. Why does he use a wheelchair, how does he go to the toilet and how does he get washed and dressed?

Rich became really sick and had to go to hospital. He was so ill that when he recovered, he couldn't use his legs anymore. People help him to get washed and dressed, and he has tubes in his stomach that help him go to the toilet.

Rich also asks the children questions: do they know anyone who's disabled? A few put their hands up. Then he points out that in every family there is someone with a disability – the most likely one being that someone wears glasses.

But Rich doesn't always go into schools to talk to children. His favourite sport is pool, and sometimes he can play as much as five hours a day. This year, in May, he had the chance to play in the world pool championships representing England, and came 16th in the world. So now he's practicing hard to go again next year to win the competition.

© 2003 Carla Moss, A&C Black Publishers Ltd

Prayer:
Dear God, thank you for giving all of us our wonderful bodies and all the things we can do with them. AMEN

34. walk in peace

Words and music by Stephen Chadwick
© 2003 Stephen Chadwick , A&C Black Publishers Ltd

1 Walk in peace through the world,
  Try to be a friend,
Walk in peace through the world,
  Let the shouting end.
Walk in peace through the world,
  Never pick a fight.
Walk in peace through the world,
  Always do what's right.

Chorus
Walk away from conflict, walk away from pain,
Pray for those who want to hurt or harm you.
Walk away from anger, walk away from fear,
Choose a better way, make a fresh start every day.

2 Walk in peace through the world,
  No more thoughts of greed,
Walk in peace through the world,
  Think of those in need.
Walk in peace through the world,
  All possessions share,
Walk in peace through the world,
  Show you really care.
Chorus

3 Walk in peace through the world,
  Don't let quarrels last,
Walk in peace through the world,
  Let the past be past.
Walk in peace through the world,
  All the wrongs forgive,
Walk in peace through the world,
  That's the way to live.

Chorus

Walk a-way from con-flict, walk a-way from pain,

Pray for those who want to hurt or harm you.

Walk a-way from an-ger, walk a-way from fear,

D.C. for verse 2 and 3 al Fine

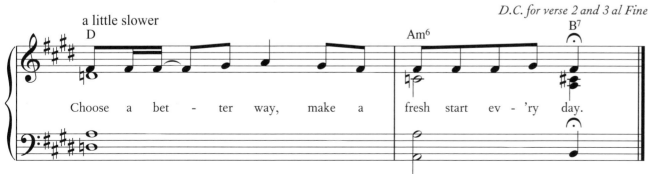

a little slower

Choose a bet-ter way, make a fresh start ev-'ry day.

Guidance notes:
A song calling for peaceful behaviour from everyone.

Christian talking point:
Jesus said in the Sermon on the Mount that anger was taken very seriously by God (Matthew 5:21-22). The Bible teaches that God judges not only our actions, but also our words, thoughts and intentions. That is why Christians ask God to help them live his way each day. What do the children think about God being as upset by their angry thoughts and words, as by their angry actions?

Talking point:
Ask the children whether they think anger is a good thing or not. Explain that anger often escalates and in the end can ruin friendships and individual lives. Perhaps discuss different ways of managing anger eg counting to 10 or talking the situation through with someone else.

Story:
Will we ever stop fighting? *by Steve Stickley*

Around Christmas 1914, thousands of young British soldiers and thousands of young German soldiers fired bullets at each other from muddy trenches. It was the First World War. The rain had been dreadful, the mud extremely deep and sticky. Then on Christmas Eve a cold frost fell and the mud froze. The soldiers woke up to a magical morning glistening in bright sunshine. No-one knows who started it, but the soldiers sang carols to one another. German soldiers sang for British soldiers, British soldiers sang for German soldiers. Silent night... Oh come, all ye faithful...

That evening, make-shift Christmas trees were put up with lights on them so that the enemy could see them from their trenches. On a snowy Christmas morning the young men who should have been fighting, climbed out of their trenches and warily made friends with their enemy.

Photographs of families were swapped, some cut each other's hair, food was shared and soldiers even exchanged bits of uniform. Someone got out a football and they had a match – dozens of soldiers enjoying themselves. As they ran around like boys their breath puffed like steam trains and their cheeks went red.

When Christmas was over, just a few days later, they went back to fighting each other again.

Prayer:
Almighty God, please help us to learn how to live with others in peace. If we feel angry, please forgive us and give us your peace. Please help us to control our anger, and help us all to find ways to make and encourage peace. AMEN

35. Peace

Words and music by Ruth Wills
© 2003 Ruth Wills, A&C Black Publishers Ltd

1 Do not be afraid my friend,
    For I made you.
Do not be afraid my friend,
    For I love you.
And whatever tomorrow may bring,
    You are safe and secure in my hands.
I will guide you and give you peace,
    I will guide you and give you peace,
I will guide you and give you peace.

2 Do not be afraid my friend,
    For I know you.
Do not be afraid my friend
    I understand you.
And whatever the future may hold,
    You are safe and secure in my hands.
I will guide you and give you peace,
    I will guide you and give you peace,
I will guide you and give you peace.

3 Do not be afraid my friend,
    I'll never leave you.
Do not be afraid my friend,
    My peace is with you.
I have promised I'll always be there,
    You are safe and secure in my hands.
I will guide you and give you peace,
    I will guide you and give you peace,
I will guide you and give you peace.

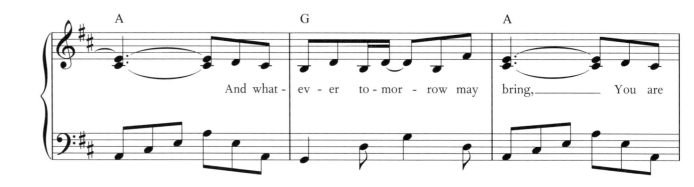

safe and se-cure in my hands._____ I will guide you and give you peace, I will

guide you and give you peace, I will guide you_____ and_ give you_

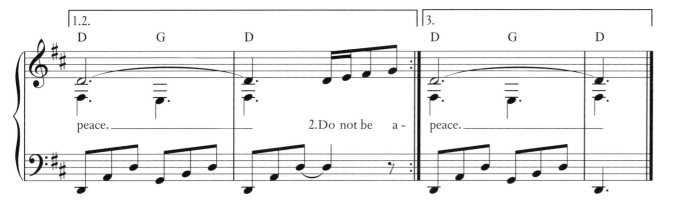

1.2.

peace.

2.Do not be a-

3.

peace.

Guidance note:
God's promise of inner peace.

General talking point:
It is hard to be at peace if we are full of fear. Yet anxiety is sometimes a good thing. It is what makes us ready to fight or run away. If we were never scared we might not duck when a falling object comes towards our head, or push our way out of a smoke-filled room. One of the ways to control fear is to make our breathing slower and deeper, and to take a few seconds to think calmly. What other ways can the children think of to cope with feelings of fear?

Reflection:
'A trouble shared is a trouble halved' – talking about something we're afraid of usually puts things into perspective. In a moment's silence, if there is something you are afraid of, think of someone you trust that you would like to share it with. Imagine what you might say.

Prayer:
Dear God, thank you that we can trust you when we are afraid. Help us to know your peace today and always. AMEN

36. morning's here

Words and music by David Stoll
© 2003 David Stoll , A&C Black Publishers Ltd

Morning's here.
　Sun shining bright
Banishes night,
　No place for fright and
No more fear.

Morning's here.
　Light everywhere
Chases out care,
　Warms up the air and
All is clear.

Let love fill your heart;
　That's the way to start.
Let love fill your mind;
　That way you will find the answer.

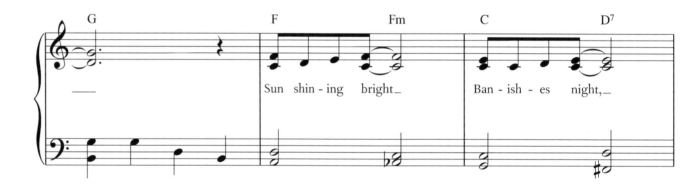

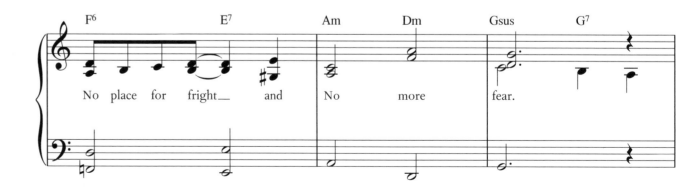

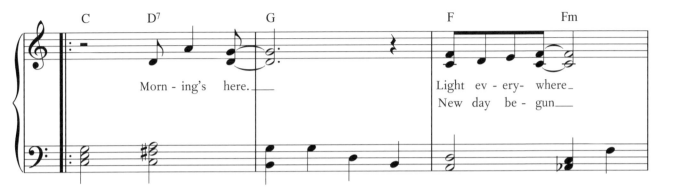

Morning's here.
   New day begun
For everyone
   Under the sun and
God is near.

Let God fill your heart;
   That's the way to start.
Let God fill your mind;
   That way you will find the answer,
God is the answer.

Morning's here.
   Everyone friends,
All hatred ends,
   Sunshine defends us
Now that morning's here.

Guidance Notes:

The message of the song is that God's love is renewed daily.

Christian talking point:

There are lots of 'mornings' mentioned in the Bible. In the description of creation (Genesis 1), after each new group of things God makes there is a new morning, a new day. Sometimes we are enjoying ourselves so much we don't want the experience to end, but at other times we can't wait for a horrible thing to be over. This song reminds us that every day is an opportunity for new beginnings and new creations.

Reflection:

With eyes closed, imagine the light chasing out everything that you are worried or frightened about. Say to yourself silently in your head, 'today is a new day, let love fill my heart'.

Prayer:

Dear God, please let love fill our hearts and our minds. AMEN

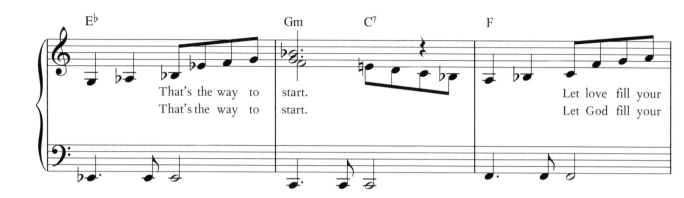

That's the way to start.
That's the way to start.
Let love fill your
Let God fill your

mind;
mind;
That way you will find the ans - wer.

That way you will find the ans - wer,

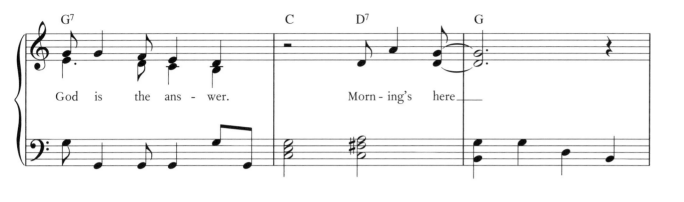

God is the ans - wer. Morn - ing's here

Ev - 'ry - one friends, All ha - tred ends,__ Sun - shine de - fends__ us

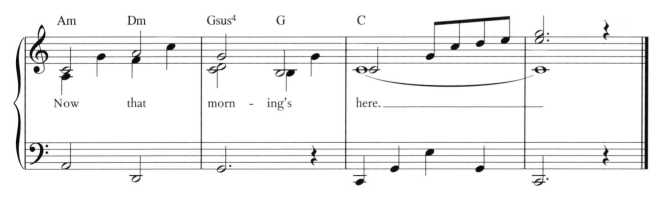

Now that morn - ing's here._____

37. Song of Blessing

Words and music by Mark and Helen Johnson
From 'Songs for Every Assembly' by Mark and Helen Johnson © Out of the Ark Music

1 May God bless our teachers,
   And all our helpers.
May God show his goodness in all that they do.
   We ask for the children
That God's hand be on them,
   And may we find his love in this school.

2 May God bless our teachers,
   And all our helpers.
May God show his goodness in all that they do.
   We ask for the children
That God's hand be on them,
   And may we find his peace in this school.

3 May God bless our teachers,
   And all our helpers.
May God show his goodness in all that they do.
   We ask for the children
That God's hand be on them,
   And may we find his joy in this school.

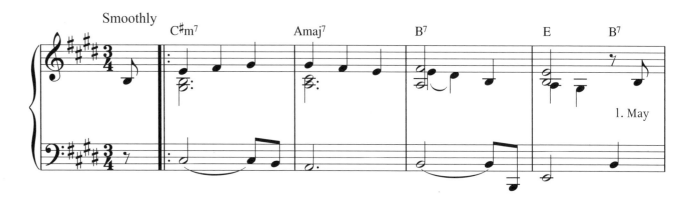

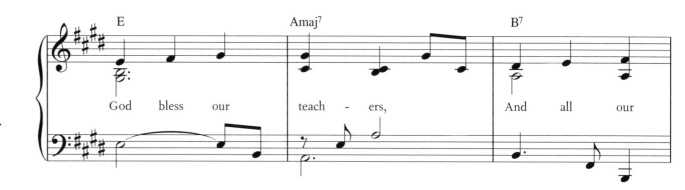

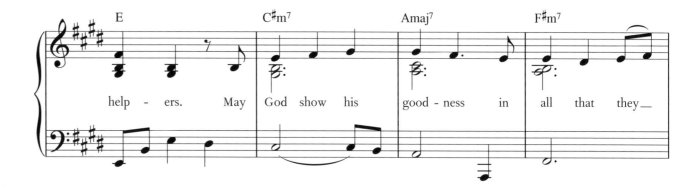

do. We ask for the chil - dren That

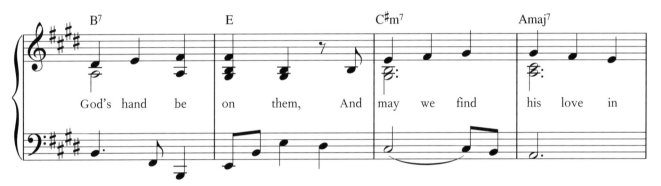

God's hand be on them, And may we find his love in

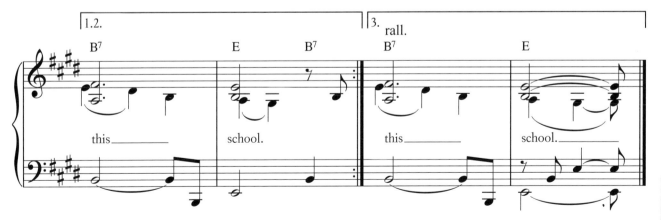

1.2. this_____ school.

3. rall. this_____ school._____

Words Psalm 23, music by Peter Readman
© 2003 Note-orious Productions Ltd , A&C Black Publishers Ltd

1 The Lord is my shepherd, I shall not want,
  He makes me lie down in pastures green,
He leads me beside the waters so still,
  And there he restores my soul.

2 He guides me down paths of righteousness
  While frightened by shadows of pain and death,
I fear no evil, I fear no pain,
  Your rod and staff comfort me.

3 My cup overflows with love from your heart,
  My head is anointed with oil from your hand,
So goodness and love are forever with me;
  I will dwell in the house of the Lord.

Guidance note:
The words are taken from Psalm 23.

Christian talking point:
Ask the children to make a fist with one hand. With one finger of the other hand they touch their thumb and say 'The'; touch the next finger and say 'Lord'; the next and say 'is'; the next and say 'my'; and lastly the little finger and say 'shepherd'. Now ask them to do it really quickly and say 'The Lord is my shepherd'. Finally ask them to imagine being held tightly in the palm of Jesus' hand. What would it feel like?

Prayer:
Dear God, please help us to trust and follow you, the way little sheep follow a good shepherd. AMEN

Guitar chords

Here are the guitar chords found in this book. In some of the songs, unusual chords have been indicated. If you can play them they will add colour and interest to your accompaniments. However, you may find it easier when they occur to substitute a common chord of the same letter name (major or minor as required). For example, the chord of C may be played where Csus^4 is marked, Am may be played for Am^6 etc.

A cross above a string means that it should not be sounded. A bracket linking two or more strings indicates that they should be held down simultaneously by the first finger.

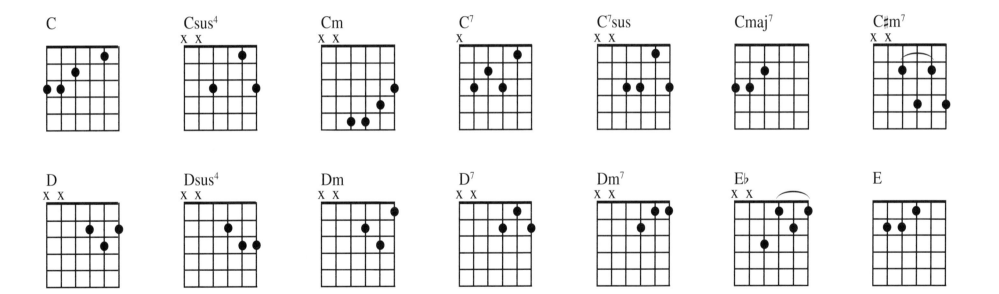

Em

E⁷

Em⁷

Em⁷⁽⁻⁵⁾

F
X X

Fm
X X

F+
X X

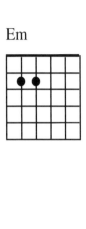
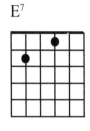
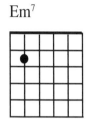
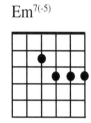
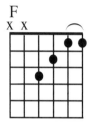
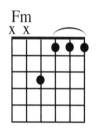
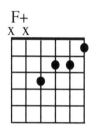

F⁶
X

F⁷
X X

Fmaj⁷
X

F♯m
X X

F♯⁷
X X

F♯m⁷
X X

G

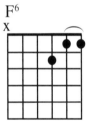
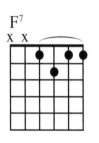
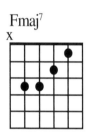
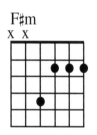
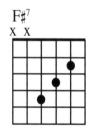
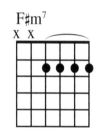
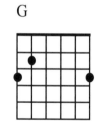

Gsus⁴
X X

Gm
X X

G⁷

Gm⁷
X X

Gmaj⁷

G♯m
X X

A♭
X X

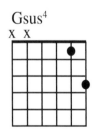
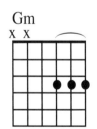
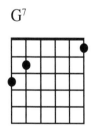
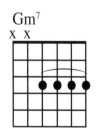
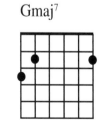
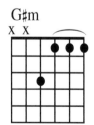
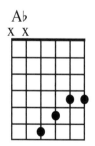

Everyone's singing, Lord • © 2003 A&C Black Publishers Ltd • Photocopying without a licence is illegal, see inside front cover

Abmaj[7]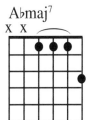

A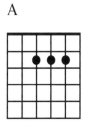

Asus[4]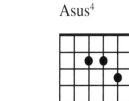

Am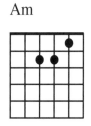

A+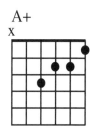

Am[6]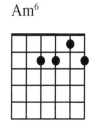

A[7]

Am[7]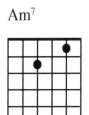

Am[7(-5)]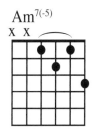

Amaj[7]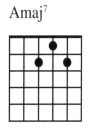

Amaj[9]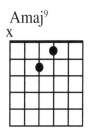

Bb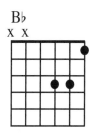

Bbsus[4]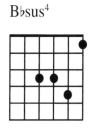

Bbm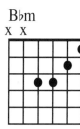

Bbm[7]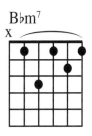

Bbmaj[7]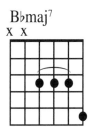

Bm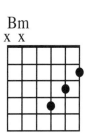

B[7]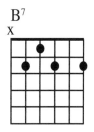

Bm[7]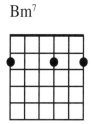

Bm[7(-5)]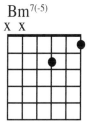

Index of first lines